Goldilocks
and the Three Bears

Retold and illustrated by Valeri Gorbachev

A Cheshire Studio Book

North-South Books

NEW YORK · LONDON

ONCE UPON A TIME, there were three bears who lived together in a little cottage in the woods. There was a great big father bear, a middle-sized mother bear, and a wee small baby bear.

One morning the three bears decided to go for a walk
in the woods while their breakfast porridge cooled.

While they were gone, a little girl named Goldilocks came
past their cottage:

She peeked in the window, and when she saw that no one
was at home, she went inside.

There on the table sat the three bowls of porridge. The porridge smelled so delicious that Goldilocks just had to have some.

First she tried the porridge in the great big father bear's great big bowl, but it was too hot.

Next she tried the porridge in the middle-sized mother bear's middle-sized bowl, but it was too cold.

Then she tried the porridge in the wee small baby bear's wee small bowl, and it was just right! So she ate it all up.

When she had finished the porridge, Goldilocks wandered into the sitting room where she found the three bears' chairs.

First she tried the great big father bear's great big chair, but it was too hard.

Next she tried the middle-sized mother bear's middle-sized chair, but it was too soft.

Then she tried the wee small
baby bear's wee small chair, and
it was just right! So Goldilocks
sat down in the chair . . .

and broke it all to bits!

Then Goldilocks went upstairs, where she found the
three bears' beds.

First she tried the great big father bear's great big bed, but it was too hard.

Next she tried the middle-sized mother bear's middle-sized bed, but it was too soft.

Then she tried the wee small baby bear's wee small bed, and it was just right! So Goldilocks lay down and fell fast asleep.

No sooner had Goldilocks fallen asleep than
the three bears returned home. Their walk
had made them very hungry, so they hurried
right into the kitchen.

Goldilocks had left the spoon in the great big father bear's porridge.

"Someone has been eating my porridge!" said the great big father bear in his great big voice.

The middle-sized mother bear saw that the spoon had been left in her bowl of porridge, too. "Someone has been eating my porridge!" said the middle-sized mother bear in her middle-sized voice.

Then the wee small baby bear looked at his bowl of porridge. "Someone has been eating my porridge!" cried the wee small baby bear in his wee small voice. "And they've eaten it all up!"

The three bears hurried into the sitting room.

Goldilocks had knocked the pillow off the great big father bear's chair. "Someone has been sitting in my chair!" said the great big father bear in his great big voice.

The pillow on the middle-sized mother bear's chair had been moved, too. "Someone has been sitting in my chair!" said the middle-sized mother bear in her middle-sized voice.

Then the wee small baby bear looked at his chair.

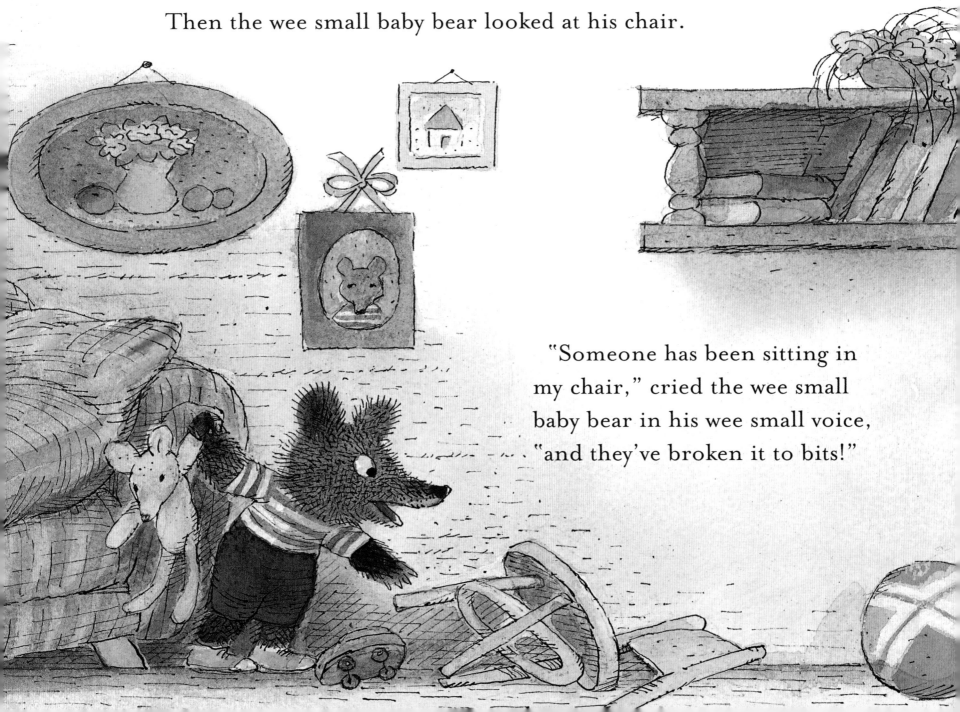

"Someone has been sitting in my chair," cried the wee small baby bear in his wee small voice, "and they've broken it to bits!"

Then the three bears went upstairs.

Goldilocks had messed up the covers on the great big father bear's bed.

"Someone has been sleeping in my bed!" said the great big father bear in his great big voice.

The covers on the middle-sized mother bear's bed had been messed up, too.

"Someone has been sleeping in my bed!" said the middle-sized mother bear in her middle-sized voice.

Then the wee small baby bear
looked at his bed.

"Someone has been sleeping in my bed!"
cried the wee small baby bear in his wee small voice.
"And here she is!"
Goldilocks woke with a start.

She leaped out of bed, jumped through the window,
clambered down from the roof, and ran away just as
fast as she could go.

What happened to Goldilocks afterwards, no one knows. The three bears never saw her again, and they lived happily ever after in their cottage in the woods.

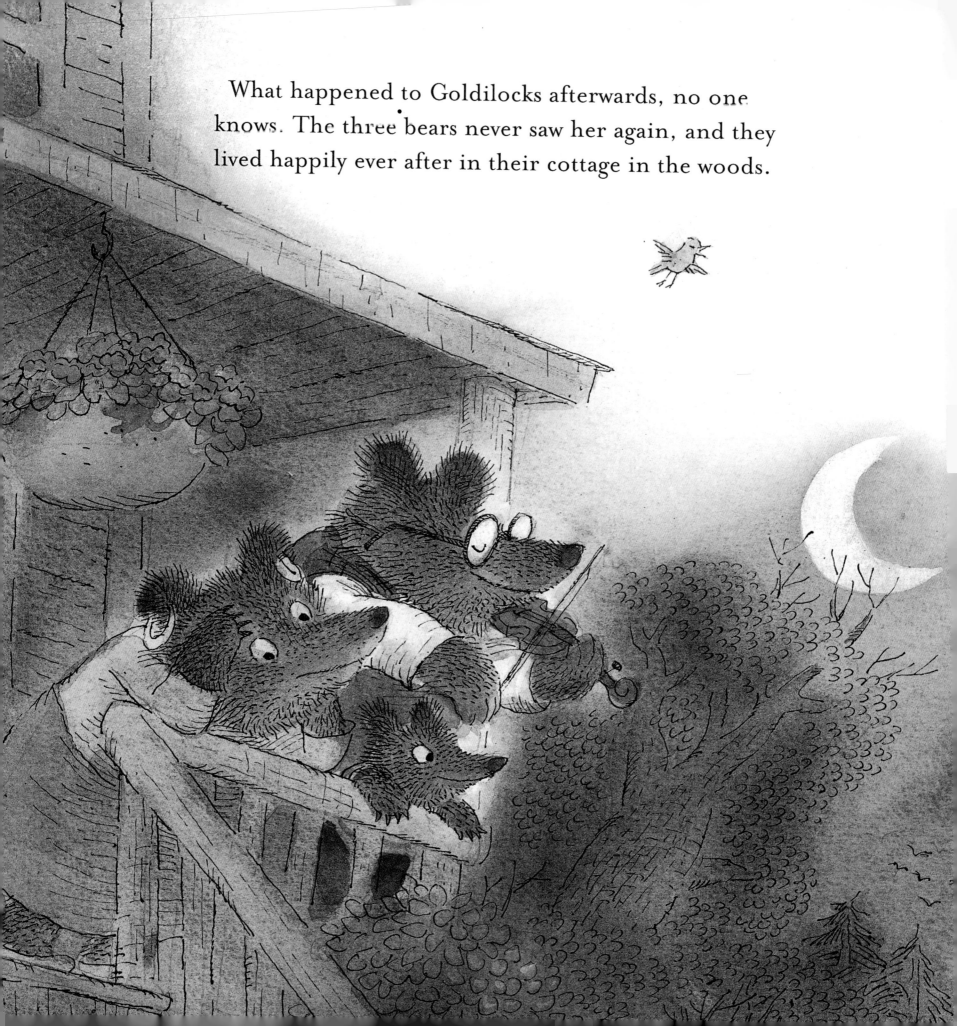

FOR MY FRIENDS

A CHESHIRE STUDIO BOOK
First published in the United States, Great Britain, Canada, Australia, and New Zealand in 2001
by North-South Books, an imprint of Nord-Süd Verlag AG, Gossau Zürich, Switzerland.
First paperback edition published in 2003 by North-South Books.
Distributed in the United States by North-South Books Inc., New York.

A CIP catalogue record for this book is available from The British Library.

Library of Congress Cataloging-in-Publication Data
Gorbachev, Valeri.
Goldilocks and the three bears / retold and illustrated by Valeri Gorbachev.
p. cm.
"A Cheshire Studio book."
Summary: A little girl walking in the woods finds the house
of the three bears and helps herself to their belongings.
[1. Folklore. 2. Bears] I. Goldilocks and the three bears. English. II. Title.
PZ8.1.G6367 Go 2001 [E] 398.22–dc21 00-064637

ISBN 0-7358-1438-4 (TRADE EDITION)
1 3 5 7 9 HC 10 8 6 4 2
ISBN 0-7358-1439-2 (LIBRARY EDITION)
1 3 5 7 9 LE 10 8 6 4 2
ISBN 0-7358-1782-0 (PAPERBACK EDITION)
1 3 5 7 9 PB 10 8 6 4 2

For more information about our books,
and the authors and artists who create them,
visit our web site: www.northsouth.com
13 14 15 V008 13 12 11 10